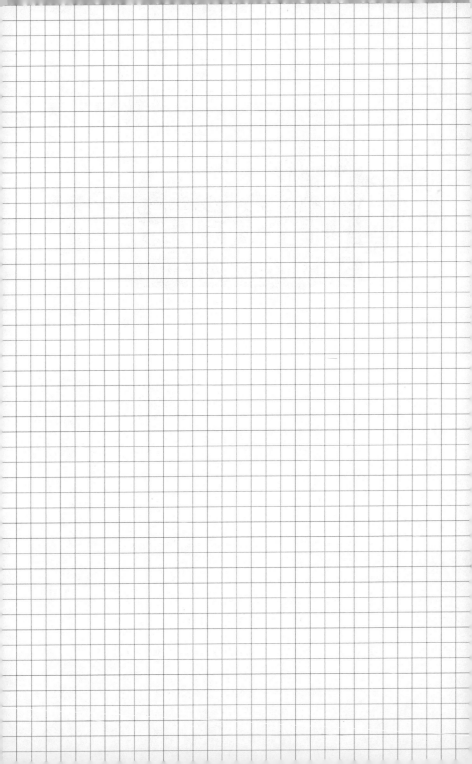

The Tinkerers

OPPOSITES ATTRACT

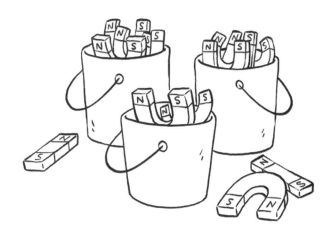

Patricia Lakin

illustrated by Valerio Fabbretti

Albert Whitman & Company
Chicago, Illinois

For my father, Samuel Miller Lakin,
an inspirational tinkerer, par excellence.
With enormous thanks to our son,
Benjahmin, a true tinkerer.—PL

To my grandparents—VF

Library of Congress Cataloging-in-Publication
data is on file with the publisher.

Text copyright © 2022 by Patricia Lakin
Illustrations copyright © 2022 by Albert Whitman & Company
Illustrations by Valerio Fabbretti
First published in the United States of America
in 2022 by Albert Whitman & Company

ISBN 978-0-8075-7955-8 (hardcover)
ISBN 978-0-8075-7956-5 (ebook)

Printed in the United States of America
10 9 8 7 6 5 4 3 2 1 LB 26 25 24 23 22 21

Design by Aphelandra

For more information about Albert Whitman & Company,
visit our website at www.albertwhitman.com.

CONTENTS

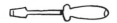

CHAPTER 1

SOMETHING MISSING

"Our home needs something," said Roscoe to his friends. He pulled his spectacles from his vest and studied the space inside the walls of Big River Junkyard.

It was hard to believe that just a few weeks ago, Roscoe the raccoon had been the only one living in the forgotten-about corner of the junkyard. Happily, it was now home to three new friends: Bart the bear, Wanda the woodpecker, and Luna the badger.

"Roscoe, you asked what our home needs,"

said Wanda. She flapped her wings and set down a can of neatly sorted nails. "It certainly does not need more junk."

Now that there were four of them living in the junkyard, Luna had insisted on organizing things. That way they could have more space for new projects.

"I'll tell you what we need," said Bart, shoveling soil onto their newly made raised vegetable garden. "H_2O."

"Is that another one of your bad jokes?" said Wanda. She hadn't known her friend for long, but she knew very well that he liked to make jokes. And that they weren't always the best.

"I believe Bart is referring to the formula for water," said Luna. She was placing books onto an old bookshelf next to Roscoe's shed. "We need to find a way to get H_2O from the river to our garden."

"Will this need more planning?" asked Bart. "I don't mind shoveling and planting. But planning makes me tired." He reached for his special walking stick, flipped down the seat, and plopped down.

"Not planning," said Luna. "We just need something to carry our H_2O."

"I know just the thing!" said Roscoe. He had found three large buckets earlier in the day. Each bucket had been filled with large pieces of metal, which he'd studied. Each metal piece was shaped like a U. The letter *N* was on one end and the letter *S* was on the other end. Roscoe wasn't sure how to use these metal pieces. But until he decided, he went and got the buckets and dumped the metal out. They were now ready to carry water.

"Wanda can carry my bucket," Bart said with a yawn.

"Not funny," said Wanda. She flew onto Bart's head and gave him a gentle woodpecker tap. "I will supervise," she said, flying off. "Grab a bucket! Let's go. What we need is H_2O!"

Roscoe unlatched their new wooden gate. After everyone was out, he gazed back at the sign he'd made weeks ago, which he'd carefully nailed to the outside of the gate. It said "Home of the Tinkerers" and had a drawing of each of them.

Wanda flew above the group as they rounded the bend and trudged down the hill. They went single file on the path that cut through the pine grove. Finally, they made it to the riverbank.

"Just think," said Luna. "When we first met, this lovely, sparkling river was a muddy, raging one."

Bart, Wanda, and Luna had come to Roscoe's junkyard after a fire had swept through their valley. After the fire, rain had poured down, causing mudslides. Big River had flooded over its banks, forcing them to find a new way to get to their food source on the other side.

"But it had a happy ending," said Roscoe. "Because of all that, we now have our beautiful bridge." He gazed at what they'd built using large wooden shutters, long lengths of rope, and a heap of clever engineering.

"Let's find a calm spot to collect our H_2O," said Luna. "The river isn't as fast as it was. But it will still push our buckets downstream."

"I'm on it!" said Wanda. She flew high up.

After a moment she found a calm inlet on the bank of the river, which none of them had noticed before. As they dipped their buckets in the water, Wanda noticed something else.

"What's that?" She pointed at the inlet. Along

the bank was a domed pile of branches, twigs, leaves, and mud. Shiny objects on the dome glittered in the sun.

Roscoe set down his bucket to take a look. "I don't know what any of it is," he said.

"Maybe those twigs and branches landed here from upstream," said Luna.

"Enough talking," said Bart. "I am anxious to water our plants." He looked up at the sky. "Sun is going down. Now is the perfect time to water."

"You mean before you take another one of your naps," said Wanda. She flew above them as Bart, Luna, and Roscoe carried their water-filled buckets.

"Easy for you to say," said Bart. "These buckets are heavy!"

"I'll sing you a song to make it easier," chirped Wanda.

As Wanda sang, the three others trudged through the pine grove, around the bend, up the hill, through the wooden gate, and into their junkyard home.

Roscoe was the last one to enter. He bolted their wooden entry gate shut. It was lovely to join his friends as they watered their new garden. And he was starting to get used to having more space. Still, as he looked up at their enormous yard, he had a feeling something was missing. He was about to ask for ideas when he heard a deafening noise.

Bang! Bang! Bang!

"Open up!" a deep voice called from the other side.

Bart, Luna, Roscoe, and Wanda froze.

"Who could that be?" Roscoe whispered to the others.

"Open up, we say!" the deep voice shouted.

"I didn't say 'open up,'" said a second, much calmer voice. "I didn't want to come here in the first place. I don't want any trouble."

"What on earth is going on?" whispered Luna.

"I think there are two of them," whispered Bart.

"I can check," said Wanda. She flew just to the edge of the fence and peeked. "I see two of them. I think they have black and white stripes," she reported back.

"Skunks! I knew I smelled something bad," shouted Bart.

"We are not, nor have we ever been, skunks. We demand to see Bart, Luna, Roscoe, and Wanda."

"How do they know our names?" said Bart, who forgot to whisper.

"How do you think?" said the one with the deep voice. "Your pictures are on the sign on this fence. You are the Tinkerers, and that is just who we are after!"

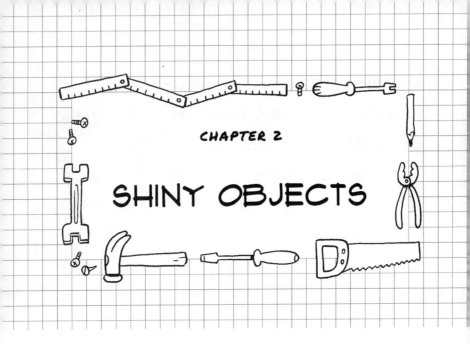

CHAPTER 2

SHINY OBJECTS

Luna peeked through a crack in the wooden gate. "I think you are beavers. Am I right?"

"You are correct," said the calm voice. "I'm Felix, and I'm with my best friend, Oscar."

"Felix, don't be nice to them," said Oscar. "Let us in!"

The second beaver shoved his body against the gate, which broke off the latch. He marched straight into the Big River Junkyard.

"Well, that's not very polite," said Wanda. "It's even destructive." She motioned to the gate's latch on the ground.

"Polite? Look who is talking about being polite. You ruined our lodge!" said Oscar. He adjusted his gray bow tie.

"Ruined your what?" Bart stood extra tall and looked down at Oscar.

"A lodge is where they live," said Luna. "That's what beavers construct at the edge of a riverbank. If the water runs too quickly, they can build dams, make a shallow pond, then build a

lodge. If I recall, you beavers are excellent engineers. Am I right?"

"Yes," said soft-spoken Felix. He removed his blue cap and took a small bow. "It's very clever of you to know so much about us beavers."

"She reads a lot," said Wanda. "But *we* did not ruin your lodge."

"I bet their lodge is that pile of twigs and branches we saw near our bridge," said Roscoe.

"Correct." Felix smiled again. "A carefully constructed pile though."

"Enough of this chatter," said Oscar. "Felix and I are here to *demand* that you clean up the junk you dumped on our home. We saw you leaving our inlet with your buckets."

"Junk?" asked Roscoe. "We were just getting water from the river."

"What proof do you have that it was us?" asked Bart.

Oscar looked around. "Proof? Here's my proof. This *is* a junkyard!"

Bart, Roscoe, Luna, and Wanda stood in disbelief.

Then Bart spoke up. "Are you lodging a complaint against us?" This time, Bart was not making a joke. He was getting upset. "I don't like to be accused."

"If I may offer a suggestion," Luna said quietly, "why don't we all go down to the river and investigate?" She smiled at Felix and Oscar.

"Horrible idea," said Oscar. "I already know you four are the culprits."

"We are not the culprits," snapped Bart. "We're the Tinkerers. That means we fix things."

"And that is what we should do, Bart," said Roscoe. "It's getting dark. I will fetch flashlights and fresh batteries so we can investigate the scene of the crime."

Oscar insisted on leading the way. He was followed by Bart, Luna, Felix, and Roscoe. As usual, Wanda flew high above.

"See what you've done?" Oscar said once they reached the river. He flashed his light onto their lodge. Pieces of metal glittered in the light.

"It does sparkle," said Wanda. "But I guess you're not into sparkle, right, Oscar?"

"Correct!" he snapped. "And I cannot tolerate a messy home."

"We certainly didn't put that stuff there," said Bart.

"But we can help you find a solution," said Luna. "If we can find out who made this mess, perhaps we can get them to fix it."

"Good idea, Luna."
Roscoe aimed his flash-
light to the ground.
"I'm sure we can find
some clues around here
somewhere."

"I'll search near the boul-
der," said Luna.

"I'll check out our bridge,"
said Bart. "There has to be
some clue about who really
did this."

"Felix, help us look
instead of gazing up at
the stars," Oscar said,
pulling him toward
the lodge.

"But the stars also
have such a lovely
sparkle to them," said
Felix.

Wanda covered the most ground. She flew over the water and along 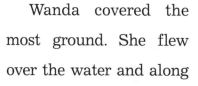 the riverbank, gripping the flashlight between her boots. "Over here!" she called after a short while.

The five of them followed Wanda along the riverbank.

"I don't see a thing." Oscar crossed his arms.

"Oh, quit grumbling," Wanda warned Oscar. "We are trying to help."

"That's what I've been trying to tell

my friend," said Felix. "If he wasn't so persnick-
ety about the metal, we could have lived with it."

"Never!" said Oscar.

"Hold it," said Bart. "I see some sparkling
things along the riverbank."

"And I found tire tracks here, close to your
lodge," Wanda said, pointing at the muddy bank.

"These tire tracks had to have been made by
a heavy truck," said Luna, aiming her flashlight
along the tracks. "Look how deep they are."

"Those sparkling things look like the same metal we have on top of our lodge," said Felix.

"And these tracks can lead us to the culprit," said Luna. "All of which leads me to a plan."

"Not another plan," moaned Bart. "I don't want to talk. I just want to show Oscar that we are not, I repeat, *not* the culprits."

"I wasn't thinking about a big kind of plan," said Luna. "This is a simple plan. I suggest we follow the tire tracks. The mud marks will make them easy to follow."

"Oh," said Bart. "That is a plan I can handle."

Roscoe gulped. Normally he liked Luna's plans. However, this one made his stomach flip. "But who—or what—will we find at the other end?" he asked.

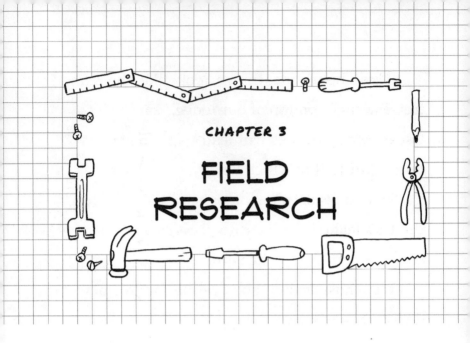

CHAPTER 3

FIELD RESEARCH

"Roscoe, stay with us," Bart called out.

"But...but..." Roscoe didn't dare admit he couldn't move. He preferred to spend his nights in the safety of his shed. Not hiking in the dark.

"Roscoe, you can say it," said Wanda. "You're scared. Well, I will protect you." She flew back to where Roscoe stood, and perched on his head. "Onward."

"Thanks," said Roscoe as he caught up with the others. "My flashlight doesn't illuminate much. And this part of the riverbank is really dark."

"This better lead to answers," growled Oscar, who walked in front of Roscoe.

"Will it lead to the lead leakers?" chuckled Bart. "Get it? Those two different sounding words are spelled the same way. Is that a pun I just made?"

"No," said Wanda. "A tongue twister and another bad joke."

"Whose idea was this, anyway?" said Oscar. "Following muddy tire tracks on this path won't lead to a thing." He turned to Bart. "And don't make another joke!"

"He won't have to," said Wanda. "I see a road up ahead."

"Thank goodness," said Roscoe. "And there

are streetlights. We can save our batteries." He flicked off his flashlight. The others did the same.

"The muddy tracks go up this road. Then they turn to the left," said Luna. "We'll follow you, Bart."

They marched single file on the side of the well-lit road.

"What if these tire tracks go on forever?" asked Felix. "We could be walking for days."

"And without one snack," said Roscoe. "Did anyone bring a snack?"

"Not me," they each said, except for Oscar. He just growled.

"See any berry bushes or trees up ahead?" Roscoe asked Wanda. He was feeling far less scared but far hungrier.

"Nothing but fields and the highway up ahead," said Wanda, who was still perched on Roscoe's head.

They marched for at least a mile.

Suddenly, Bart froze. "Look!" he called.

"What?" They crashed—each one falling into the one in front of them.

Bart got up slowly, brushed himself off, and explained. "The tire tracks head off to the right. They go onto this narrow, hilly road," he said.

"Why did you have to scare us like that?" asked Oscar as he brushed off the dirt from his bow tie. The others brushed themselves off without a word.

"I see a truck parked at the top of the hill," said Wanda. "The tracks seem to lead straight to it."

"More climbing?" asked Bart. "And me coming on this adventure without my portable seat? But..." He looked at Oscar. "If that's what it takes to prove our innocence, I'll march."

As they rounded the corner at the top of the hill, Oscar was the first one to spot the sign. "It says, 'Home of W & W Nut and Bolt Factory.'"

"Aha! Now we're getting down to the nuts and bolts of this mystery," said Bart. He turned, looking for a reaction to his joke.

"Sorry, Bart. But we are too tired to laugh," said Felix. "Let's see if anyone is in the factory."

"All the windows are dark," said Roscoe.

"I'll check it out," said Wanda. She flew to the side of the building. In a flash, she was back. "Two men—in the basement—quick—crawl on your bellies so they don't see us."

"Why?" asked Felix. "We don't know that they are the cause of our mess."

"Well, it wasn't us," said Bart. "And this *is* the home of a nuts-and-bolts factory, the very objects lodged in your lodge."

"True," agreed Felix. He shoved his cap into his back pocket. "All right, let's get down and crawl."

"I refuse to ruin my bow tie," Oscar said as he flipped the bow tie to face behind him.

Finally, the five of them landed on their bellies and crawled to the side of the building where Wanda directed them to go.

"Shhh!" said Wanda. "Don't make a sound. Let's hear what they are saying."

"Looks like they are arguing," said Felix. "Just like you argue with me, Oscar. Maybe they are best friends too," he added.

"Hmmph!" was all Oscar said.

"Wally, I told you not to turn on that particular

switch on the nut- and bolt-making machine," said the man. The name *Willy* was embroidered on his shirt.

"Okay! So now I reread the directions, and I saw what our mistake was."

"Our mistake, Wally? It was *your* mistake."

"Well, what about your mistake?" said Wally. "I told you to take the truck filled with the ruined metal stuff and dump it at the Big River Junkyard.

That's where it belonged. What did you do, Willy? You dumped it in the Big River!"

"I didn't hear the junkyard part, okay?" said Willy.

"So now what do we do?" asked Wally.

"Forget about it! They're sunk in the river. From now on we can finally sell what we are supposed to make—screws with threads, nails with heads, and nuts with holes in them," said Willy. He looked up. "Hold it! I heard a noise. Someone is out there!"

"Where?" Wally's gaze followed where Willy's finger pointed.

"Up there, right outside our window," said Willy. "Let's go see!"

"What do we do now?" whispered Felix to the others.

"GO! GO! GO!" said Bart as he, Luna, Roscoe, Wanda, Felix, and Oscar tore down the hill.

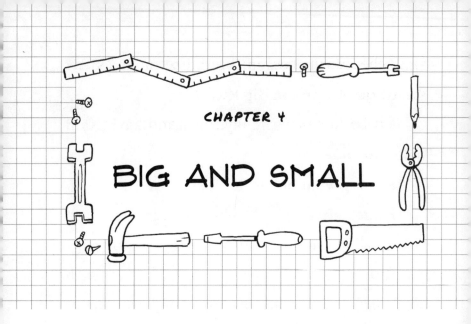

CHAPTER 4

BIG AND SMALL

The group scrambled away as fast as they could and in seconds made it to the highway. Luna was the one who spotted the headlights from the W & W truck.

"They're barreling down on us," she said as the truck's headlights grew brighter and came closer and closer.

"Quick! Hide behind these bushes." Bart held back the branches that draped the side of the road.

The rest of the crew did as Bart directed. They

scrunched down behind the thicket of trees and stayed quiet.

"I'll be lookout," whispered Wanda. She flew to the top of a tree.

After a minute, she reported back. "They've just passed this very spot."

"What if they turn around and come back this way?" asked Felix. "How will we get back home?"

"Good question," said Luna. "We should get off this road. If we walk home between the riverbank and the junkyard, they won't spot us. That is, as long as they don't drive their truck off this road."

"Luna's right," said Oscar. "Let's follow her advice."

"Good for you, Oscar. You said that without a grumble," said Wanda. "And now I hope you know who the true culprits are."

"Indeed," said Felix. "I'm sure you agree, Oscar."

Oscar simply nodded. He and the others followed Luna across the road. Then they scrambled under tree limbs and around bushes until they found themselves between the riverbank and the fence of Big River Junkyard.

 In the distance, there was a loud grinding noise that sounded like it was coming from the junkyard. Wanda flew over the fence to investigate, but in the dark, she

could not see what had made
the unusual sound.

"There is no way Willy
and Wally can find us here,"
said Roscoe. Although, he
wasn't sure he believed his
own words. "Right?"

"I don't think so," Luna
said as they reached Oscar
and Felix's inlet. "It's starting to rain. Let's sit
together in the pine grove and ask ourselves some
questions."

Roscoe took shelter under a pine tree. He
didn't like the rain one bit!

"I have a question," said Bart. "Who is tired
and needs to go to sleep?" He answered his own
question. "ME!"

"But Luna is right," said Wanda. "We've just
had a scary encounter. We need to figure some
things out so we can actually *get some sleep*."

"Exactly," said Roscoe. "Coming up with a

plan always helps me calm down."

"Well, I have a plan," said Oscar. "We know who messed up our lodge. But it still needs to be cleaned up. And I think Wally and Willy should do it."

For a moment, no one spoke. None of the others wanted to go anywhere near the W & W Nut and Bolt Factory again.

"I have another idea," said Luna. "We didn't cause the problem, but we can help you fix it. That's what the Tinkerers do."

Roscoe and Wanda nodded. They would be happy to help their neighbors.

Bart gave a sigh. "Okay, as long as we don't have to go back to that factory again."

"Great!" said Luna. "The first step is to know what the problem is."

"That's easy," said Oscar. "Our lodge is a big mess!"

"I have to agree," said Felix.

Roscoe looked at the lodge. Small pieces of metal glittered in the moonlight. "That is the big problem, but there's a little problem too. Those nuts and bolts are small."

"Roscoe is right. My paws aren't made to pick up such little things," said Bart. "I will supervise while you all pick up."

Oscar crossed his arms. "I will not have anyone trampling on top of our lodge. It could cave in!"

Felix nodded. "The last thing we need is to build a new lodge."

"So we need a way to pick up the metal pieces without stepping all over the lodge," said Luna.

"That is the problem. Now we just need to find the solution."

"Now we need to go to sleep," said Bart.

"I'm with Bart," said Wanda. She turned to Felix and Oscar. "Let's meet tomorrow morning at our junkyard. Knowing Luna and Roscoe, they'll have come up with a plan by then."

And so Felix and Oscar returned to their lodge, and the others made their way back to the junkyard.

Wanda flew to her perch and nestled down. Bart returned to his cave and curled up. Roscoe tucked himself into his cozy, warm bed with his drawing pad. Luna lay in her tunnel and read. And everyone in Big River Junkyard fell asleep hoping morning would bring a solution to their problem.

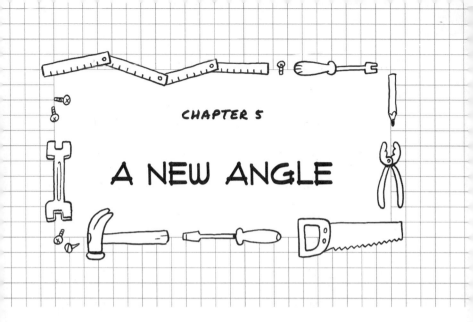

CHAPTER 5

A NEW ANGLE

Sure enough, as the sun came up the very next morning, Luna greeted everyone with a huge smile. On the drawing table, she had collected nails, spools of wire, scissors, tape, and batteries.

"What on earth is all this for?" asked Oscar.

"I was thinking about our problem," said Luna. "We can't pick up the metal pieces ourselves, or we'll walk all over your lodge. So we need something else to pick them up for us."

Felix scratched his head. "How do we do that?"

"We can use magnets!" she said.

This time it was Bart who scratched his head. "And how do we do that?"

Luna pointed to an object she had put together. "We take a long nail. Then we wrap the wire around it many, many times. We take one end of the wire and tape it to one end of a battery. We do the same with the other end of the wire. It gets attached to the other end of the battery."

"Does that battery and wire-wrapped nail actually do anything?" asked Oscar. "Or is it some silly sculpture?"

Sculpture? Roscoe wondered why Oscar would say that. He was about to ask him, when Wanda asked for everyone's attention.

"Please listen," said Wanda. "Let Luna finish."

"Thank you," said Luna. "The battery sends electrical energy through the wire to the metal nail. The moving electricity, or current, creates a magnetic field. The nail then becomes an electromagnet that can attract other metal things — like your nuts and bolts!"

Roscoe looked at the object in disbelief. "That is a magnet?" he asked. "How strong is it?"

"The more wire we wrap around the nail, the stronger the magnetic pull will be," said Luna.

Oscar was not impressed. "That is all fine," he said. "But you still have a big problem. How will you use them without stepping on our lodge?"

Luna shrugged. "I have not figured that part out yet."

Bart spoke up. "Maybe Wanda could fly over the lodge and use the magnet to pick up the nuts and bolts."

But Roscoe had a better idea. He pulled out the drawing he had made the night before. His idea was nothing like Luna's, but it could help.

The drawing showed Roscoe by the river with a long stick and a string attached to the end.

"Roscoe, are you fishing in your drawing?" Wanda asked.

Roscoe shook his head. "Not exactly," he said. "I thought we could use fishing rods to pull the little pieces up. That way we wouldn't walk all over the lodge. I wasn't sure how to get them to stick, but..."

"If we attach the magnet to the end of the string, we can go magnet fishing!" Luna broke out into a huge smile.

"I get it!" said Wanda. "We stand on the shoreline with our fishing magnets, reach over, and clean up Felix and Oscar's lodge."

"Yes!" Luna smiled. "That's the plan."

Felix nodded. "That is a very clever plan."

Everyone looked at Oscar.

"Fishing? Magnets? You are all full of silly ideas," he said. "I have a mind to go find Wally and Willy and demand they clean up their metal trash."

Oscar got up, marched through the open gate, and stormed out.

"No!" cried Wanda. "We have to stop him!"

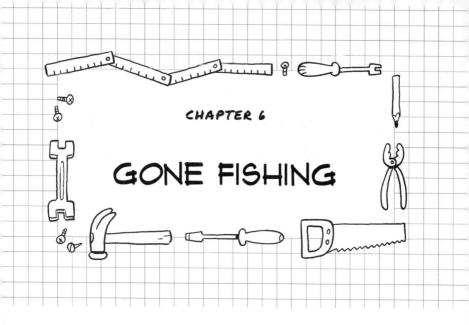

CHAPTER 6

GONE FISHING

"I'm his best friend. Maybe I can stop him," Felix said, hurrying after Oscar.

"I hope Oscar doesn't find Wally and Willy," said Roscoe. "They meant to dump their metal mistakes in *our* home. What if they had landed right on top of our garden?"

"All the more reason we need to get busy," said Wanda. "Let's make some magnets."

"First let's make sure this homemade magnet works," said Bart.

"I like your scientific thinking," said Luna.

45

"Make a plan and try it out first. The metal on your suspenders can be our test."

"We can call this the Suspenseful Scientific Suspender test." Bart chuckled as Luna held the magnet next to the metal clasp of his suspenders.

"The joke is on us," said Wanda. "The magnet is barely sticking."

"Oh no." Luna buried her face in her hands. "I really thought this magnet idea would work. Now we will never be able to clean up Oscar and Felix's lodge."

"It's only a failure if we don't learn from it," said Roscoe. That was what Luna had told him the first time one of their ideas didn't work. "Maybe there is another magnet we can use."

Luna looked up and smiled. "Thanks, Roscoe."

She unzipped her backpack, took out a book, and opened it to a bookmarked page. "I did read that there are different types of magnets. We made one using electricity—an electromagnet. But there are also permanent magnets. Those can be much stronger."

Luna pointed to a picture of a piece of metal in the shape of a U.

"Wait! Are those magnets?" Roscoe put on his spectacles and studied the photo. "We have those very same magnets right here in our own junkyard! They even have the same *N* and *S* letters on them!"

"Where?" asked Luna, Bart, and Wanda all at once.

"They were stored in the buckets we used to carry water from the river," said Roscoe. He scooted off and returned minutes later with other containers filled with different-sized magnets.

"The big ones will work best for our fishing magnets," said Bart. "And look at how it sticks to my suspenders!" He had to yank the magnet away.

"Yeah! These magnets are strong enough! Let's get busy," said Wanda. She spread out string and gathered sturdy sticks to make fishing rods.

Bart attached one end of the string to a stick. He secured the other end of the string to the curved part of a magnet. He placed the finished magnetic fishing rods on the table.

"Look at that!" said Bart. "We knew these magnets worked. But look how strongly these two are sticking together."

"Not these two," said Wanda. "It feels like some invisible force is pushing them away from each other."

"That's exactly what's happening," said Luna.

"But why do the magnets do different things—pulling together or pushing apart?" asked Roscoe.

"It's what I've been studying," said Luna. "Each magnet has two sides, or poles. *N* stands for 'north pole' and *S* stands for 'south pole.' If you try to put two of the same poles together, it feels like they're pushing each other apart."

"So the ones pushing away from each other have the two south poles close together," said Wanda. "It would be the same if both north poles tried to touch."

"Correct," said Luna.

"And the magnets that stick together have a north pole touching a south pole. Is that right?" said Wanda.

"Yes," said Luna. "Opposites attract."

"Are we talking about Felix and Oscar?" asked Bart. "Felix sure seems like a positive one, and Oscar sure is the negative one. Maybe that's why they stick together."

Roscoe, Luna, Wanda, and Bart broke out laughing.

"Not a joke, but a clever observation," added Roscoe.

They grabbed their fishing poles and headed for the river.

"Yes!" Luna cheered when she spotted Felix and Oscar together. "I guess Felix was able to hold Oscar back from going to Wally and Willy's factory."

"Grab a pole," Wanda told Oscar and Felix.

"We are going magnet fishing, and we'll clean up your lodge as easy as one, two, three!"

When they each had a rod, they headed for the riverbank.

"I'll supervise," Wanda said as she flew above the lodge.

"Supervising?" muttered Bart. "That's just another name for getting the easy work."

"Well, if you can fly above our heads and direct the magnetic fishing rods, then go ahead," said Wanda. She tapped her foot. "I'm waiting."

"Okay, okay," said Bart. He adjusted his suspenders, grabbed his fishing pole with its dangling magnet, and headed for the lodge.

"Okay, everyone," said Wanda, "at the count of three, lower your rods. And aim right where my beak is pointing."

They did exactly as they were told. Even Oscar.

"I've got a bolt," said Luna.

"I've got two nails," said Roscoe.

"I've got three screws," said Bart.

"I've got four springs," said Felix.

"I've got a headache," said Oscar. "You're all just fiddling with those silly magnetic fishing

rods. They will not be able to clean up all the metal on top of our lodge."

"I don't agree with all of Oscar's opinions," said Felix. "But he is correct about the cleanup. It will take a very long time with these magnets."

Roscoe didn't always agree with Oscar either. But something Oscar had said earlier kept nagging at him. What was it? *Oh well*, he thought, and he listened to Luna instead.

"I know we need to learn from our mistakes," said Luna. "But I thought these magnets would do the trick. Oscar is right. Even these more powerful magnets are not strong enough. We need a mega magnet."

"How can we make one of those?" asked Roscoe.

"I'm not looking to do any more tinkering," said Bart. "We've done enough."

"We don't need to *do* anything," said Oscar. "We must demand that Wally and Willy clean it up."

"No way!" said Bart, Roscoe, and Luna at the same time.

"Those nincompoops will only cause more trouble," Roscoe added. Above him, Wanda was squawking and flying in circles.

"Live with the metal on your lodge," said Bart. "You could use it for…"

"For what?" Oscar yelled. He waved Wanda away as she tried to land on his head. "I want

that metallic mess out! You all may not have put it there. But you sure don't know how to clean it up either."

"I don't often agree with what Oscar says," said Luna. "But sadly, I think he's right. We don't know how to create a magnet powerful enough to clean up this mess."

"Luna! Roscoe! Bart, Oscar, Felix!" squawked Wanda. "Listen to me!"

But none of them were in the mood to listen.

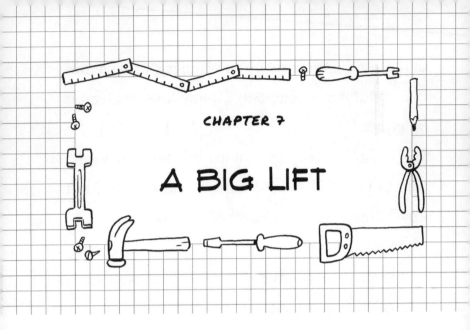

CHAPTER 7

A BIG LIFT

"You've *got* to listen to me," said Wanda. She beat her wings and circled her friends. "I think I know how to clean up Oscar and Felix's lodge."

"Not another plan." Bart sighed.

"No," she said. "It is something I saw in our very own backyard."

"What?" asked Roscoe.

"It started with that noise we heard last night in the junkyard," Wanda said. "I went to look for it this morning, and I didn't believe what I saw. It was this giant piece of metal attached to a crane.

I saw that metal lift up...Are you ready?"

"Tell us!" said Bart. "You saw it lift up what?"

"I saw it lift up an entire car!" said Wanda. "I didn't know what it was at first, but now I know it must have been a magnet."

"Get ready, folks!" said Roscoe. "That's our answer! Let's go find that mega magnet in our own backyard."

As they entered Big River Junkyard, Oscar asked, "Where is it? Where is this magnetic crane?"

"I'm trying to remember where I was flying when I saw it," said Wanda.

"I remember read-ing about this kind of magnet in my book," said Luna. "It gets its power from electricity, like the battery magnet I made, except it's much, much bigger."

"I saw some old car parts behind my cave," said Bart. "Maybe that's where it is."

"Good thinking," said Felix. He turned to Bart. "Lead the way, please."

Bart took them behind the metal hut that made up his cave. On the other side was a high

wooden fence that led to a whole other section of the junkyard. He undid the latch and pushed open the gate. Bart turned to Oscar and said, "This latch reminds me that you still need to fix the one you broke on our front gate."

Oscar didn't answer. He and Felix were busy staring at what was before them.

"Well, will you look at that!" said Felix. "I've never seen so many cars—all shapes and sizes. Here are some squashed as flat as a pancake."

"I don't often fly around this section of the junkyard," said Wanda. "But here is where I saw that crane. Now all we have to do is find it."

"Doesn't a crane have a cab where the driver sits, and a big arm that sticks up?" asked Roscoe. "Let's look for that sticking up part."

"The crane's arm could have been left close to the ground," said Luna. "Let's spread out and start our search."

"First one to spot the crane should yell out, 'Magnet!'" said Bart.

"You mean *electromagnet*," said Luna.

While Wanda flew above them, Felix, Oscar, Bart, Luna, and Roscoe went their separate ways.

Roscoe decided to head for the pancake-like squashed cars. But after searching up, down, around, and through the flattened cars, he found no sign of a crane. He was about to check on the others when he heard Wanda squawking loudly.

"You didn't call out, Oscar! You didn't tell us!" Wanda screeched.

Roscoe ran to where Wanda and Oscar were. Oscar sat in a rusted-up cab. A tarp covered part of the cab. Attached to the front was the crane, resting on the ground. It was no wonder they'd had a hard time finding it.

Roscoe spotted Wanda flapping her wings at the cabin's open door.

"Get away," Oscar shouted at her.

"He doesn't know Wanda," Roscoe said to the others, who had all gathered when they heard the commotion. "She's not easily dismissed."

"I can work this all by myself," shouted Oscar.

He undid his bow tie and slipped on a pair of goggles that had been hanging on the cab's door handle.

Whirr! Oscar had done something that started the motor. "Let me just see what switch does what to lift the crane," he added.

Slowly, they watched a big yellow metal arm lift up, higher and higher. At the end of the arm, a giant gray metal slab was attached. Wires ran from the slab all the way down the arm of the crane.

"Here," Bart said. He lifted up an unattached car door. "See if you can get the magnet to lift this."

"Just hold it up!" said Oscar. "I have to figure what switch does what."

"I am holding it," said Bart, lifting the door a bit higher.

Whoomp! In seconds, the electromagnetic block sucked the door high into the air. Bart clung to the door handle. He too was swept high into the air and left dangling high above their heads.

"Hey!" shouted Bart. "I can fly like you, Wanda. Now I can supervise." Then he looked down. "Oh no! Get me down!"

"Oscar, what did you do?" cried Luna.

"Put Bart down right now!" Wanda stamped a red boot on the top of the cab's roof. "No, don't!" she said suddenly. "Friends, we need to make sure Oscar puts Bart down carefully *and then* releases the magnet."

"Exactly," said Luna. "Otherwise, Bart will get…" Luna stopped talking. "I can't even think about it."

"Let me in that cab," demanded Wanda. "I will help with the controls."

Oscar did exactly as Wanda instructed. She chirped out instructions while sitting on Oscar's shoulder. In seconds, the crane moved to the left.

Slowly, it lowered, getting closer and closer to the ground. Bart clung to that door handle with all his might. The car door was glued to the giant magnet.

In a few seconds, Bart was finally touching the ground. "Safe to let go?" asked Bart, who had covered his eyes.

"Yes!" they all shouted.

Bart let go, bent down, and kissed the ground.

"Make room for the car door," said Wanda. "Oscar, move this lever to where it says 'Drop.' That shuts off the power and, well, everyone just watch."

Sure enough, the metal was no longer magnetized. *Clank!* The car door dropped.

"Thank goodness no one was hurt," said Luna. "And now, thanks to Wanda, we know how to work the crane *and* activate the magnet."

"Excuse me," corrected Oscar. "But I can also handle this crane. If you want to help by assisting me, that's fine. Or *supervising*, as you call it."

"Fine with me, Oscar," said Wanda. "We'll work together to move this crane into place. Okay, friends?" she asked the others.

"Fine with us," they all said.

"And now, thanks to Bart and his test run, we know this mega magnet works," said Luna.

With Wanda and Oscar as a team, they got the crane into place in no time. They positioned the metal block right over Felix and Oscar's lodge.

"Ready, set..." Wanda directed Oscar to turn on the magnet.

"STOP!" Luna froze. "We can't do this."

"Why not?" said Wanda. "Everything is ready for the clean-up."

"I just realized we have a huge problem," said Luna.

Bart folded out his seat and slouched down. "I don't think I can deal with any more problems."

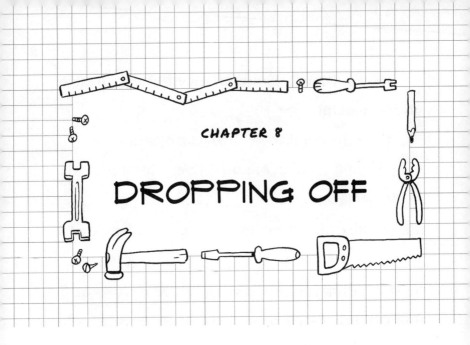

CHAPTER 8

DROPPING OFF

"I will try to stay calm," said Wanda. "Luna, what is our problem?"

"Where will we put all that metal once we clean up Oscar and Felix's lodge?" asked Luna. "That is our problem."

"Well, first take it from our lodge," said Oscar. "Then dump it in the river, far, far away from us."

"No way!" said Wanda.

"That's not solving the problem," said Luna. "It simply passes the problem on to someone else. In addition—"

"In addition," Roscoe added, "*None* of us wants to pollute the Big River."

"Exactly," said Felix. "We should protect our habitat."

"And keep other habitats safe and clean," added Bart.

"I get it! I get it!" said Oscar. "Well, then let's just dump it in Wally and Willy's yard. They dumped it here. We should give it back to them."

"That's not right," said Luna.

"Why not?" asked Oscar.

"Two wrongs don't make something right," said Roscoe. "That's why."

"While we are arguing about what to do with all of this metal, my lodge is covered with Wally and Willy's mistakes," said Oscar. "So let's do something."

"Well, I do think we should come up with a plan," said Luna.

Bart sighed. "Here we go again. I must say, I am almost agreeing with Oscar. I don't want to come up with a plan. I want action."

"We all want to see this magnetic machine clean up Oscar and Felix's lodge," said Wanda. "But once we do that, we still have to decide what to do with all that metal."

"You call yourselves the Tinkerers," said Oscar. "You take the metal back to your place! Fix things with it! Build something! I'm sure you can make something totally silly."

"Build something silly," Roscoe said quietly.

"Wait a minute, Oscar. I am remembering when you said something else was silly."

"What did I say?" asked Oscar. "I can't remember half of what I say."

"You said something when Luna showed us how to make our own magnets," said Roscoe. "I felt like your words planted an idea in my head. But I kept forgetting what it was—that is...until now." Roscoe smiled.

"What's your idea?" asked Luna.

"I think I need to plan it out first," said Roscoe. "At least I should draw a prototype."

"A prototype will not clean up my lodge," said Oscar. "I'm getting tired just sitting in the cab of this crane without being able to turn any knobs or rev the engine!" Oscar adjusted his goggles.

After a moment, Roscoe said, "Okay, I agree with Oscar."

"You do?" asked Bart. "You agree with everything he says?"

"Not everything," said Roscoe. "But I do agree that we should turn on our magnet and clean up his and Felix's lodge. Afterward, we'll bring the crane with the metal attached back to our junkyard. My idea will put Wally and Willy's big mistake to good use."

"I trust Roscoe," said Luna. "We should proceed."

"Is the clean-up a go then?" asked Wanda.

Everyone agreed, so Wanda helped Oscar place the magnetic metal block above the lodge.

"Okay," said Wanda. "The magnet is in position. Now you need to move the lever inside the cab to where it says 'Lift.' That will turn on the magnet. Ready, set, go!"

Oscar did exactly as he was told. *Wamp!* In seconds, metal bits flew from the lodge and glopped onto the magnet.

"We did it!" they all cheered.

"Okay," Wanda directed. "Now let's get us, our

magnetic crane, and the metal mess safely back to our home."

"Let me guess," said Bart. "You'll supervise?"

"Yes!" said Wanda. "You are learning." She flew above them and guided the giant crane back into its rightful place.

"Let's drop the metal into our wheelbarrow for now," said Roscoe.

Everyone agreed. And with Wanda's help, Oscar guided the magnet just above the plastic wheelbarrow.

"Now lower the crane," directed Wanda. "When the magnet is just above the wheelbarrow, move that lever to 'Drop.'"

"Done!" said Oscar. He climbed out of the cab. "I for one want to go back home, now that our lodge has been cleaned up."

He headed for the open gate.

"No way!" the others said at once.

"We went to all this trouble to clean up your lodge," said Bart. "The least you can do is help with Roscoe's plan…whatever it is."

Wanda squawked and circled Oscar's head, while Bart, Luna, Felix, and Roscoe stood side by side, blocking the gate.

CHAPTER 9

MISSING
NO MORE

Oscar tried dodging them. But it was hard with Wanda pecking at his head.

"I give up," Oscar said finally. "Besides, I am a bit curious about how I planted an idea in your head, Roscoe. What was my idea?"

"I mentioned that it was something you said," Roscoe explained.

Oscar shrugged. "Sometimes I just say whatever pops into my mind."

"Well, I'm glad one of the thoughts that popped out of your mouth is what popped into my head.

78

You gave me a great idea," said Roscoe.

"Really? Me?" Oscar looked confused.

"Yes," said Roscoe. "It occurred when Luna was showing us how to make magnets."

"That magnet-making attempt was a bust," said Oscar.

"Not really," said Wanda. "We did make a real magnet. It just wasn't strong enough."

"And we always learn from our mistakes," Luna added.

"Roscoe, please tell us what we do with this mess." Bart flipped open the seat on his walking stick and plunked himself down.

"It will be quick," said Roscoe. He'd taken out his drawing pad, put on his spectacles, and uncapped his drawing pen. Roscoe began to hum as he worked.

"Oh, this is going to be wonderful," he smiled.

"I hope so," said Wanda as she flew above him and tried to peek.

"No fair," said Roscoe. "I will show you all the second I'm done...which is...now!" He held up his drawing.

"It's a monster," said Bart.

"It's a mess," said Oscar.

"It's a metal mountain," said Wanda.

"It's a sculpture!" said Roscoe. He turned to Oscar. "That's what you thought Luna was making when she tinkered with the nails, wire, and batteries. You asked if it was a silly sculpture."

Luna studied Roscoe's drawing. "This is very clever. You've got a wooden base and some wooden posts sticking up. I see those U-shaped magnets in your drawing too. Are they all attached to the wooden posts?"

"Yes!" said Roscoe. "We can nail the wooden pieces together and tie on the magnets to the wooden posts. Then we let the magnets do their work. The metal objects will be placed wherever we want. They will stick to the magnets. It could be an ever-changing sculpture."

"Why do we need that?" asked Bart. "A mound of metal is not art."

"Well, it can be art. Art is not something one needs," said Roscoe. "But it makes life a lot more interesting. Remember how I said I thought something was missing from our home? That was it! And thanks to Wally and Willy and Oscar and Felix, we have a mound of metal to tinker with."

"I think it is a wonderful idea," said Luna. "Look at what we've gained just from knowing some things about magnets."

Oscar began to walk off, carrying two of the magnets.

"Hold it, Oscar," said Bart. "Where are you going with those magnets?"

"Where do you think?" Oscar looked up. He was actually smiling. "I am using the magnets to fix the gate I broke. And I listened. I know to put opposite poles together so the latch will actually close your gate."

"Well, well, Oscar," said Luna. "Welcome to the world of the Tinkerers."

"I think the sculpture should be near our

82

vegetable garden," said Bart as he adjusted his suspenders. "Let's get busy. We have art to create."

While Oscar worked on the latch, Felix, Luna, Roscoe, and Bart gathered long wooden posts. Wanda brought over a can full of nails.

With their hammers, they made a wooden base. Then they nailed wooden posts here and there along the base's four standing sides. Then they tied the magnets at different points along the standing wooden posts.

"Now let's create!" said Roscoe. He scooped up some metal from the wheelbarrow and gave it a gentle toss. "See! It's sticking! We are magnetic artists!"

Soon they were all scooping up the metal from

the wheelbarrow and tossing it onto their magnetized posts.

"This is a magnificent magnet party," said Bart.

"You're right," said Wanda. "It is a party. But
like Roscoe realized long ago, something is missing. I know just what it is too. I'll be right back."

The crew was too busy tossing the metal onto the magnets to notice how long Wanda was gone.

"Surprise," Wanda called when she flew back, carrying a basket. "We need to celebrate our new garden, our new sculpture, and our new friends. And that calls for something sweet."

She lowered the basket to the ground, and it was full of delicious berries from their favorite tree across the river.

"Thank you, Wanda!" Luna cheered.

"And thank you, Roscoe, Bart, Luna, and Wanda, and you too, Felix," said Oscar. He looked up at the sculpture they'd just created. "It does sparkle nicely."

"And it was just what Big River Junkyard needed," said Roscoe.

Then the six of them feasted on the berries before it was time to say good night.

THE DESIGN PROCESS

It can take a lot of creativity to build a solution to a problem. By following the engineering design process, the Tinkerers make sure they are putting their creative ideas to good use.

STEP 1 Figure out the problem

Every engineering project begins with a problem. The Tinkerers need to find a way clean up Felix and Oscar's lodge without trampling all over it.

STEP 2 Design a possible solution

The next step is to come up with an idea for solving the problem. Luna suggests they try to pick up the steel pieces with magnets.

STEP 3 Build and test a prototype

The Tinkerers test out Luna's first magnet prototype on Bart's suspenders.

STEP 4 Evaluate the prototype's performance

The magnet Luna creates works. But the pull isn't be strong enough to clean up the lodge. From this, they decide they need a stronger magnet.

STEP 5 Present the results

Engineers take knowledge from each prototype and go back to Step 1. After their first prototype, the Tinkerers work on solving their new problem by using stronger magnets.

INVISIBLE ACTION

Magnets are objects with an invisible power. Every magnet is surrounded by a magnetic field. When a metal like iron, nickel, or steel (which has lots of iron in it) comes close—*whomp!*—the magnetic field acts on it. This action is called a force, and like the force of gravity pulls things down to Earth, the force of magnetism pulls certain metals together.

The same metals that are affected by magnets can be turned into magnets themselves. If you rub a magnetized piece of iron onto an unmagnetized piece, the second piece will start to become magnetized too.

So what makes a magnet different from other pieces of metal? A magnet has two poles, or ends. The magnetic field runs between the north pole and the south pole. If you hold two magnets together, opposites will attract. A north pole will pull toward a south pole, and a south pole will pull toward a north pole. Meanwhile, two north poles or two south poles will repel, or push apart.

MAGNETS EVERYWHERE

Magnets are all around us. They're used in vacuum cleaners, computers, cars, and much more. The biggest magnet on the planet is right below our feet. Earth itself has magnetic poles, which compasses use to help us find our way.

Roscoe and the Tinkerers need a magnet strong enough to clean up Felix and Oscar's lodge. For this, they use an electromagnet. Electromagnets use electricity to make their magnetic fields. Luna makes a simple electromagnet with a steel nail, some wire, and a battery, but it isn't strong enough. To get the job done, they need a mega magnet.

One good thing about electromagnets is that they can be very strong. Another is that unlike a piece of magnetized metal, an electromagnet's magnetic field can be turned on and off. This is how the Tinkerers get Bart safely to the ground— and how, in the end, they safely drop off their metal mess.